What do you know about the Phoenix – apart from the fact that it's hard to spell?

Did you know that people were talking about this astonishing bird as long ago and far away as Ancient Egypt? They believed that the Phoenix was first seen in Arabia and that it never lived for less than 500 years. Towards the end of its life, so the story went, it would build a nest of spice branches and set it alight, dying in the flames. Then, a new Phoenix would arise from the ashes.

People in China and Japan believed that the arrival of a Phoenix was the sign of a new age, or the birth of a great emperor. Just imagine, for thousands of years people from Egypt to Japan and all the countries in between, keeping their eyes open for a glimpse of this fabulous Phoenix!

ANNA and BARBARA FIENBERG

ANNA and BARBARA FIENBERG write the Tashi stories together, making up all kinds of daredevil adventures and tricky characters for him to face. Lucky he's such a clever Tashi.

KIM GAMBLE is one of Australia's favourite illustrators for children. Together Kim and Anna have made such wonderful books as *The Magnificent Nose and Other Marvels*, *The Hottest Boy Who Ever Lived*, the *Tashi* series, the *Minton* picture books, *Joseph*, and a full colour picture book about their favourite adventurer, *There once was a boy called Tashi*.

First published in 2008

Allen & Unwin
83 Alexander Street
Crows Nest 2065
Australia
Phone: (61 2) 8425 0100
Fax: (61 2) 9906 2218
Email: info@allenandunwin.com
Web: www.allenandunwin.com

Cataloguing-in-Publication details are available
from the National Library of Australia
www.trove.nla.gov.au

ISBN 978 1 74175 474 2

Cover and series design by Sandra Nobes
Typeset in Sabon by Tou-Can Design
This book was printed in December 2011 at McPherson's Printing Group,
76 Nelson St, Maryborough, Victoria 3465, Australia.
www.mcphersonsprinting.com.au

10 9 8 7 6

www.tashibooks.com

Tashi

and the
PHOENIX

written by
Anna Fienberg
and
Barbara Fienberg

illustrated by
Kim Gamble

ALLEN&UNWIN

'There's a surprise for you in the garden,'
said Mum, when Jack and Tashi walked into
the kitchen.

'Good or bad?' asked Jack.

'Sometimes it's hard to tell,' sighed Mum,
mysteriously.

There was a loud bang from the garden,
then a roar. Both boys jumped.

'That could be a lion tamer with a gun,' whispered Jack, peering out.

'Or a warlord with a temper,' said Tashi nervously. But he straightened his shoulders and went outside with his friend.

A thump came from inside the shed, followed by a crash and a very bad word. The boys opened the door just as a big hot hairy creature shot out.

'Uncle Joe! You've grown a beard!' cried Jack.

'You come back right now and put your tools away!' came Dad's voice from the shed. 'Always the same, ever since we were kids!'

'What were you doing in the shed?' asked Tashi.

Joe hugged the boys and put a hand on their shoulders. 'I'm inventing an absolutely fantastic musical instrument for my dear friend Primrose. Unfortunately my hammer slipped and caught your father's thumb.'

'Have you come to stay?'

'Well, a few days, that's if...'

'Then maybe you should get back in there,' suggested Jack, 'and help clean up.'

When Joe had disappeared inside the shed, Jack grinned. 'I like it when Uncle Joe comes to stay. But he never gives us much warning.'

'In my experience,' said Tashi, 'surprises can be tricky things. Especially surprises with uncles in them.'

'Oh, like that uncle of yours, Tiki Pu!' frowned Jack.

'Yes, he used to make me *so* angry –'

'Wait a sec, tell it when Dad comes out. A story will put him in a good mood.'

When everyone was sitting comfortably, and
Dad had stopped muttering at Uncle Joe
(even passing him the biscuits), Tashi began.

'It was like this,' he said. 'One day I was
so angry I thought I was going to explode!
I ran out of the house, across the fields and
into the forest –'

'What made you so mad?' asked Jack, his
mouth full of biscuit.

'Did someone go into your shed and mess
with all your tools and hit your thumb and
then run *off*?' asked Dad. Joe hid his face in
his cup of tea. When he looked up, his beard
was dripping.

'No, it was worse than that,' said Tashi. 'My Uncle Tiki Pu had been up to his old tricks again. He wasn't just annoying – no offence, Uncle Joe – he was *dangerous*. And this time, he put our whole family at risk.'

'So what did he do?' asked Uncle Joe.

'He's *coming* to that,' said Dad. 'Let him tell the story *his* way.'

'I was only saying –'

'Well, there I was,' Tashi put in, 'boiling with fury, running blindly, when suddenly I found myself at the entrance to a small cave.

'The air was very still, and at my feet were the embers of a fire. Two logs still glowed red and their branches were furry with ash. As I watched, the ash beneath the logs began to stir. Flashes of colour glowed through the grey: red, gold, purple, emerald, like jewels. Was treasure buried under there?'

'Well, was there?' cried Joe.

'Wipe your beard,' said Dad. 'Every time you shake your head, drops fall on my plate. In fact, why have you stopped shaving? You look like a werewolf.'

'What was under the logs?' asked Mum.
'*Treasure?*'

'No,' said Tashi. 'Or at least, not the usual
kind. Something was moving in the embers.
A bird with a tail like sunrise! I watched it
step right out of the dying fire and preen
itself.

'"Oh, how beautiful you are!" I cried. "Why weren't you burned in that fire?"

'The bird looked at me thoughtfully for a moment. "I am a Phoenix," he said calmly. "We Phoenix don't burn. In fact, every five hundred years we are born again in flames." He smoothed an emerald feather lovingly, turning this way and that to get a good view of himself. "Don't you *love* the new me?"

'"Yes," I told him, because it was true. Already I was thinking that perhaps here lay the answer to my troubles. "You are a miracle," I said. "You're as magnificent as fire itself! I remember Wise-as-an-Owl telling me once about you. Did you know that you have your own page in the Book of Spells? It says *Phoenix have eyes of crystal and tail feathers of gold*." I couldn't help my own eyes opening wide. His unearthly beauty made me feel strangely hungry, with a longing for some taste I would never have. "Oh fabulous Phoenix, you could be the very person to help me with a terrible problem."

'The Phoenix instantly drooped. He closed his eyes with boredom. "Why should I?" he asked.

'"As an act of kindness?" I suggested. The Phoenix hunched his wings disdainfully. "You are so beautiful," I coaxed, "that I would like to call you Glorious One – or Glory for short."

'"As you like," he said, "but I still haven't time to help you. That's not what we Phoenix are for. Anyway, I'll be leaving in the morning, as soon as my colours have deepened."

'I decided right then to stay by his side all night. I knew my mother would be worried, but she'd understand if my plan worked the way I wanted.

'In the morning I made one last try. "Glory, what do Phoenix like best?"

'"Hmm, I can only tell you what I would like above all else."

'"Yes? What?"

'"To feel a mother's love."

'I drew a deep breath. "If you help me with my trouble, Glory, I promise that you will have your wish."

'The Phoenix settled down in the ashes. "Tell me," he said.

'"Well, it's like this," I began. "I have an uncle, Tiki Pu, who will say anything to get out of a tight spot. This morning he came sidling into our house looking guilty, as well he might. We knew straight away that something was wrong."

'"What have you done now, Tiki Pu?"
my father sighed.

'"There's no need to look at me like
that," sniffed Tiki Pu, "as if I'm *always*
making trouble. It's just, see, I was asked
to spend the evening with the Warlord and
his friends. They were all boasting about
how many splendid horses and houses they
had. I simply couldn't stand it." He stopped,
embarrassed, and then went on with a rush.
"And so I told them that on my last voyage
to Africa I had captured the most dazzling
creature in the world. That was good – they
all looked crestfallen."

' "But then the Warlord said, 'Where is this creature? I want to see it!' Well, I hadn't thought of that, and in my confusion, I'm afraid I told him that I had given it to my dear family. Well, you know the Warlord. He said, 'I want this creature brought to me by tomorrow at noon, otherwise –' Tiki Pu didn't say what *otherwise* was, but you can be sure it will be the end of my family. Glory, we don't have anything like this dazzling treasure to give the Warlord. I don't know what we can possibly do."

'The Phoenix cocked his head to one side as I began to explain my plan. Then he interrupted crossly. "We Phoenix are not born to be some Warlord's plaything. We must be free to soar the heavens and dazzle the stars. What you are asking would be very undignified, Tashi." His feathers ruffled in outrage.

'"It would only be for such a little while," I explained, and I told him the second part of my plan. He quite liked the idea of astonishing the Warlord with his beauty. His feathers calmed as I talked and finally he agreed to come home with me. Besides, he was curious to meet Tiki Pu.

'I sat myself on his back amongst those
fabulous feathers and a few minutes later we
were sitting beside my amazed family at the
dinner table. Tiki Pu revived like a thirsty
plant when he saw the Phoenix and heard
my plan. He showed not a moment's worry
for the danger he had brought to the family,
and could only talk of the riches the Phoenix
would bring to him. Glory looked at him in
wonder. "He is even worse than you said,"
he whispered in my ear.

'We found a large cage for Glory and spent some time coaxing him to step into it. "This is not at all the sort of thing we Phoenix are used to," he said, looking down his beak.

'At noon the next day we were in the
Warlord's Great Hall. When he saw Glory,
the Warlord jumped up from his gold chair
and clapped his hands. He threw Tiki Pu
and me a coin each and waved us away. He
could look at nothing but the flame-coloured
feathers of the Phoenix. As we were leaving
the hall I said to the Warlord, "You do
understand, my Lord, that my family has
given up a great prize for you?"

'"Yes, yes," he replied. "In fact you and your
uncle must stay for the banquet I'm holding
tonight. I'm going to show off this fabulous
creature to all my friends and enemies."

'That evening, Glory in his cage was the
centre of attention in the Great Hall. He
preened and bowed as the guests marvelled
and told each other tall tales of Phoenix
they had almost met. His feathers glowed
so intensely, he looked like a small trapped
sun. It hurt my eyes, and my heart, to look
at him. I checked once more for the small
package wrapped in silk in my pocket.

'Towards the end of the evening, I bent
under the table, pretending to look for
something I'd dropped. In the darkness,
amongst people's fine leather boots, I drew
out my silk handkerchief. I undid the knot
and took out the squashed piece of ghost
cake. Then I stood up and strolled over to
Glory. Quickly, quietly, I dropped the ghost
cake on the floor of Glory's cage.

'He nodded to me and gobbled it up with
his ruby-red beak. Then he stepped through
the bamboo bars that melted away at his
touch. I couldn't help laughing with relief as
I watched him.

'But what was he doing now? He froze, looking back at the cage in wonder. He was entranced by the magic of the ghost cake. To my horror he stepped back into the cage and out again through the bars – in and out, again and again.

'And then, instead of flying straight for the open windows as we had planned, he glided up to the heavy gold chandelier hanging over the Warlord's chair. From there he dropped a deposit on the Warlord's head! That's the kind of bird Glory is – he just has to show off and make mischief!

'The Warlord sat shocked and silent as something white and smelly trickled down his cheeks and into his ears.

'Glory dived and tipped a flask of wine over one tipsy guest, and knocked a large bowl of vegetables over another. He was having such a good time, he didn't notice the Warlord and his men hurry over to lock all the doors and windows.

'Too late, Glory realised what he had done. I had told him the magical effects of ghost cake did not last long. He flew wildly around the room, pushing in vain at the high windows. He flashed me an anguished look. *Serves you right!* I felt like shouting, to teach him a lesson. *I warned you to be quick!*

'The Warlord and his guests were rushing about the hall throwing cloaks and tablecloths in the air like washing flapping in the wind, trying to bring the Phoenix down.

'I made my way over to the far wall and felt in my pocket for ghost cake crumbs. Nothing. Panic was making me hot all over. Breathe deep, I told myself. Carefully I drew the scrunched handkerchief out of my pocket. I smoothed it in my palm. There! One last crumb, tucked into a fold of silk. Just then someone grabbed my arm, jerking me off balance. "Quick, give me the cake!" hissed Tiki Pu.

'My fist closed tightly over the crumb. "No, I promised Glory no harm would come to him." I pulled away, waving my hand to Glory, and threw the crumb up into the air.

'Glory wheeled back but the crumb was
falling faster. He dived right down like
something about to crash, his beak pointed
at the earth, then suddenly up he swooped.

Oh, he was so beautiful, like a shooting star.
He caught the cake in his beak and then,
without a check, he sailed on through the
great stone wall and out into the freedom of
the frosty night.

'The Warlord stormed over to us. "You cheating bamboozlers!" he raged. "You have shamed me in front of my guests! You'll pay for this!"

'Tiki Pu sank to his knees, whimpering. He was going to be no help, as usual.

'"But, Sir, there is no shame," I cried. "You have given your friends – and enemies – a night to remember! Just look about you!" The Warlord turned. Indeed, his Great Hall had never been so lively. People were laughing and shouting and pointing, waving their arms in the air as they described to each other what they had just seen. "This will be a story to tell their children and grandchildren in years to come."

'Just then a guest slapped the Warlord on the back. "Well, old friend," he gasped, "What a night this has been! You have shown us not only a fabulous Phoenix, but a Phoenix who flies through walls!" And he slurped another glass of wine to celebrate.

'The Warlord looked stunned, but he smiled stiffly and nodded to the guards to push open the doors and windows. He glared at Tiki Pu, but made no move to stop us as we quickly made our way outside where Glory was waiting in the branch of a plum tree.

'When we reached home, Glory looked around expectantly. "Well, what about your promise, Tashi?"

'I glanced over my shoulder at my mother, who smiled shyly. "I promised you would feel a mother's love," I told him. "Well, this is a mother – *my* mother – and believe me, Glory, she is so grateful for what you have done for us that she will love you like her own for the rest of your days."

'At that, my mother held out her arms and Glory flew right into them.'

Dad cleared his throat. He wiped his eyes. 'Ah yes, family. Nothing like it.' He looked at his brother Joe. 'Can't get used to the beard though. Suppose it will just take time.'

Joe blew his nose. 'Like a few days?'

Dad grinned and Mum got up to clear away the tea things. Jack saw her lean down to whisper in Tashi's ear, and kiss his cheek.

'What did she say?' Jack asked Tashi when they were outside.

'She said the Phoenix might have been *my* treasure, but I happen to be *hers*.'

'Well, you're mine too,' said Jack, standing up and spreading out his arms, 'and this whole family's, and this whole *world's*!' He went running around the garden until Tashi tackled him and Jack flipped Tashi over with an ancient wrestling move taught to him by his father, who'd been taught by *his* father, the famous World Champion Suburban Lawn Wrestler.

THE UNEXPECTED LETTER

'What a surprise!' said Mum, as she opened a letter telling her that she'd won a luxury car from a lottery in Nigeria. 'Especially as I didn't even buy a ticket.'

'Life is full of surprises,' Uncle Joe told Jack.

'But they can turn out well or not so well,' said Jack, 'depending on what you *do* with them.'

Uncle Joe scratched his head. 'How do you mean?'

'Well, Tashi was talking about that very thing today.'

'Ah, I would have liked to have heard *that* conversation,' said Uncle Joe.

'Me too,' said Dad, coming into the kitchen.

'And me,' said Mum, handing him a tea towel.

'Well, it was like this,' said Jack, settling himself on a stool. 'There was a letter for Tashi. An unexpected letter –'

'*That's* not surprising,' said Uncle Joe. 'I get letters all the time. Mostly from the bank, which is bad news.'

'Well, it was surprising for Tashi. Nobody could remember such a thing happening before. The postman got off his bicycle and waited to hear what it said. All the family crowded around to see. But when Tashi had read the letter, all he said was, "I'm sorry, I can't tell you about it now. This letter has already taken four days to get here and a friend of mine is in terrible trouble. I have to go straight away."

'His mother picked up the envelope that Tashi had dropped on the table. It was of the finest paper and was addressed in rich black ink by a delicate hand. The handwriting belonged to Princess Sarashina. And it looked like it had been written in a hurry.

'Tashi read the letter again in his bedroom.

Dear Tashi, it said. Something dreadful has happened. My father the Emperor has suddenly announced that my sister, Princess Hoiti-Toiti, must marry Khan! You may not remember him, Tashi. He is the son of the Master of Revels, and for all the years we have known him he has been sneaky and cruel – I could tell you such stories! Besides, Hoiti-Toiti loves Cha Ming, who is good and kind, and loves her back.

My father won't talk about it anymore. He just keeps saying Khan will do very well – and the wedding will be held next week! I know that you and Hoiti-Toiti have not always got on together in the past, but you are the only person I can think of, dear Tashi, who might find a way to help. Please come quickly!

'Tashi shuddered as he put down the letter.
How could he forget the Master of Revels?
He'd met him only the year before, and –'

'Nearly lost his feet!' cried Dad, almost
dropping his tea towel. 'That villain was
going to chop them off!'

'That's right,' nodded Jack. 'But Princess
Sarashina sounded so worried that Tashi felt
he must go to her. Quickly he stuffed some
ghost cakes into his pocket, together with
a balm for spider bites, plus a new herb
Wise-as-an-Owl gave him for calming snakes.
Then he put on his dancing shoes and told his
family he would be back as soon as he could.

'When he arrived at the Palace, Tashi went looking for the Princess Sarashina and her sister. As he stole through the ornamental gardens he heard a voice he knew well: it was the Master of Revels. He was talking to his son Khan, and what Tashi heard next filled him with anger and dread. He moved closer, holding his breath to hear better.

'"I don't know," the Master of Revels was saying. "If the Emperor should find out..."

'Khan interrupted sharply. "He won't know a thing until it's too late, Father. I have already spread stories around the Palace that the Emperor is growing feeble-minded. People are talking. As soon as I am married I will declare that he is no longer fit to rule, and the throne will be mine – I mean ours," he quickly corrected himself.

'The Master of Revels shook his head. "We'll need more men. Too many of the Palace guards will stay loyal to the Emperor."

'"Yes, I know," Khan said impatiently. "That's why I have written this letter to General Xeng telling him to come at once with extra men."

'A troop of guards came marching past, and Khan told one of them to get a horse and deliver the letter. When the guard asked the way to the General's fortress, Khan shouted, "You fool! They'll tell you at the stables." Then he kicked the man in the bottom to hasten him on his way.

'Tashi, treading softly, keeping to the shadows, followed the guard. While he crept along, a cunning idea came to him. By the time the guard arrived at the stables, Tashi had worked out a plan. He bowed politely before the guard, and told him what was in his mind.

'That done, he hurried back to the Palace, searching through hallways,

skirting around piles of wedding presents
that guests had sent ahead, listening at doors,
until he finally heard the Princesses' voices.
Their door was locked. Of course – they
were in disgrace.

'Tashi swallowed a piece of ghost cake
and glided into the room. There was a loud
argument going on.

'" – and so there's no point in your trying to escape," Princess Sarashina was crying. "You'd be brought back to the Palace before you could say fried chicken feet, and Cha Ming would probably lose his head."

'"Then what do you suggest? Just sit here, waiting for the wedding and a life of misery with Khan?"

'The sisters jumped when they noticed Tashi standing beside them.

'"Where did you come from?" gasped Princess Hoiti-Toiti.

'"Tashi, at last!" cried Princess Sarashina, leaping up to hug him. "The wedding is tomorrow. Can you possibly help us?"

'Tashi blushed and glanced over Princess Sarashina's shoulder at Hoiti-Toiti. She was rolling her eyes. Still bossy and proud, thought Tashi. She had a fine sense of her high place in the world, and didn't really like her sister's friendship with Tashi, who had a lot of relatives but not one at the Palace.

'Tashi sighed. "Look, this is what we could do," he said quietly. And he told the sisters of the conversation he had overheard that morning in the garden, and about Khan's plans for the Emperor.

'"But how can we prove it?" Hoiti-Toiti objected. "My father would never believe a common boy like you over the son of his most trusted adviser."

'Tashi's ears flushed red and he wished yet again that this Princess had a nicer way of talking, even if he had to admit that she was right. "I spoke with a Palace guard on the way to the stables," he managed to answer calmly, "and persuaded him to let me have Khan's note to General Xeng."

'Princess Sarashina's eyes opened wide. "How did you do that?"

'"It wasn't very difficult. The guard had already decided to look for a new master, and when I explained how grateful the Emperor would be to have this warning about Khan's plan, he was only too happy to leave the note with me."

'"I knew you would think of something, Tashi!" Princess Sarashina beamed. "Now we must find a way for you to get close enough to speak to my father. There is to be a big pre-wedding dinner tonight, you know."

'"Yes, but Khan and his guards would never let me into the Banquet Hall." Tashi looked thoughtfully at the sisters. Then his eyes dropped to the beautiful carpet on the floor. He smiled. "I've just had another little idea. But first you must tell me where I can find Cha Ming.'"

'Cha Ming had never eaten ghost cakes before, and he was very surprised when Tashi pulled him through the Palace wall. Princess Hoiti-Toiti ran to her beloved Cha Ming. "Not now," said Tashi. "Cha Ming and I have some arrangements to make. We'll be back in time to escort you both to the banquet."

'The girls were dressed ready for the evening when Tashi and Cha Ming returned. Princess Hoiti-Toiti tugged Cha Ming's arm. "Make him tell us what is going to happen," she cried.

'Tashi's eyes twinkled. He flopped down on the silken carpet at his feet. "All right, Cha Ming, roll me up." The young man took one end of the carpet and rolled Tashi right up in it. "You see," Tashi's voice came from deep inside, "Cha Ming is going to deliver a beautiful last-minute present to the Emperor for his daughter."

'And that's exactly what happened. They went ahead to the Banquet Hall, where five hundred guests were already waiting. Cha Ming followed, with Tashi tucked inside the carpet like a prawn inside a dumpling. At the huge iron doors they were met by two Palace guards with swords gleaming at their sides. But one of them smiled quickly and looked down at the carpet, giving it a nod. Cha Ming smiled back. The guards waved them inside and then went before them, calling, "Make way! Make way!"

'When Cha Ming stopped in front of the Emperor's chair, he slipped the carpet from his shoulder and unrolled it across the

floor with a flourish. Out popped Tashi, like a seed from its pod.

'The air was almost whooshed from the hall as five hundred guests gasped. Khan sprang up and signalled to his men. Tashi was ready. He stepped forward and bowed, holding out the letter to the Emperor.

'"Gracious Majesty, your friends at the Court have heard that your life is in danger. Please read this letter."

'The Emperor's face froze as he read Khan's letter to General Xeng. Khan's hand clutched at his sword. His jaw clenched hard as steel. But he was too late. Tashi's new friend, the Palace guard, had already doubled the Emperor's troops and they were surrounding the hall. Khan and his father were seized and marched outside.

'The Emperor shook his head. "I can't believe it. He seemed such a fine young man." He looked over to Princess Hoiti-Toiti. "I'm sorry, my daughter. You were right and I was wrong." He gave a sad laugh. "And all the wonderful wedding preparations wasted, all the beautiful presents must be sent back…"

'The Emperor shrugged, and cleared his throat. "Well, young Tashi, once again I must ask how I can reward you for such a great service to me and my family."

'Tashi took a deep breath. "Thank you, Majesty. What I would like most of all would be to see the Princess Hoiti-Toiti marry the man she loves – Cha Ming." And he added in a rush, "The wedding could still take place tomorrow, and all the preparations would not be wasted and the presents not sent back."

'The Emperor looked startled. Then he gave a reluctant laugh. "Is that what you really want, Hoiti-Toiti?" His daughter nodded, her smile gleaming wide in the lamplight.

'"Then let the celebrations begin … *again!*"

Later that evening, Princess Hoiti-Toiti pulled Tashi aside. She took a magnificent gold medallion from her neck and clasped it around Tashi's. "I want you to wear this, Tashi, as a token of my gratitude and as a sorry from me for all the times I spoke unkindly to you in the past. I am very lucky that you have such a generous heart."

'Tashi found it hard to speak just then. There was a lump in his throat – it was the first time Hoiti-Toiti had ever been kind to him.

'He was saved from answering by Cha Ming, who laughed, "And if you were wondering what to give us for a wedding present, Tashi – there's nothing we'd like more than one of your special ghost cakes!"'

Jack's family was quiet for a moment,
thinking.

'So what's the message here?' said Uncle
Joe. 'The next time I get a bad surprise,
I should roll myself up in a carpet?'

Dad was frowning. 'I can see how the ghost cakes were useful, but what about the balm for spider bites and herb for calming snakes? Where do they come in?'

'That's another story, I bet,' said Mum.

'Or,' said Dad, his frown clearing, 'they're like the extra cash I put in my pocket when I go out for the day – a just-in-case Tashi thing.'

'A you-never-know Tashi thing.'

'A Tashi weapon-against-bad-surprises!' cried Uncle Joe, leaping up with satisfaction and dashing out to the shed.

'No, you'll see, they'll turn up in another story,' Mum whispered to her teacup. 'And it'll be a surprise.'